Loui and the Grass Tree

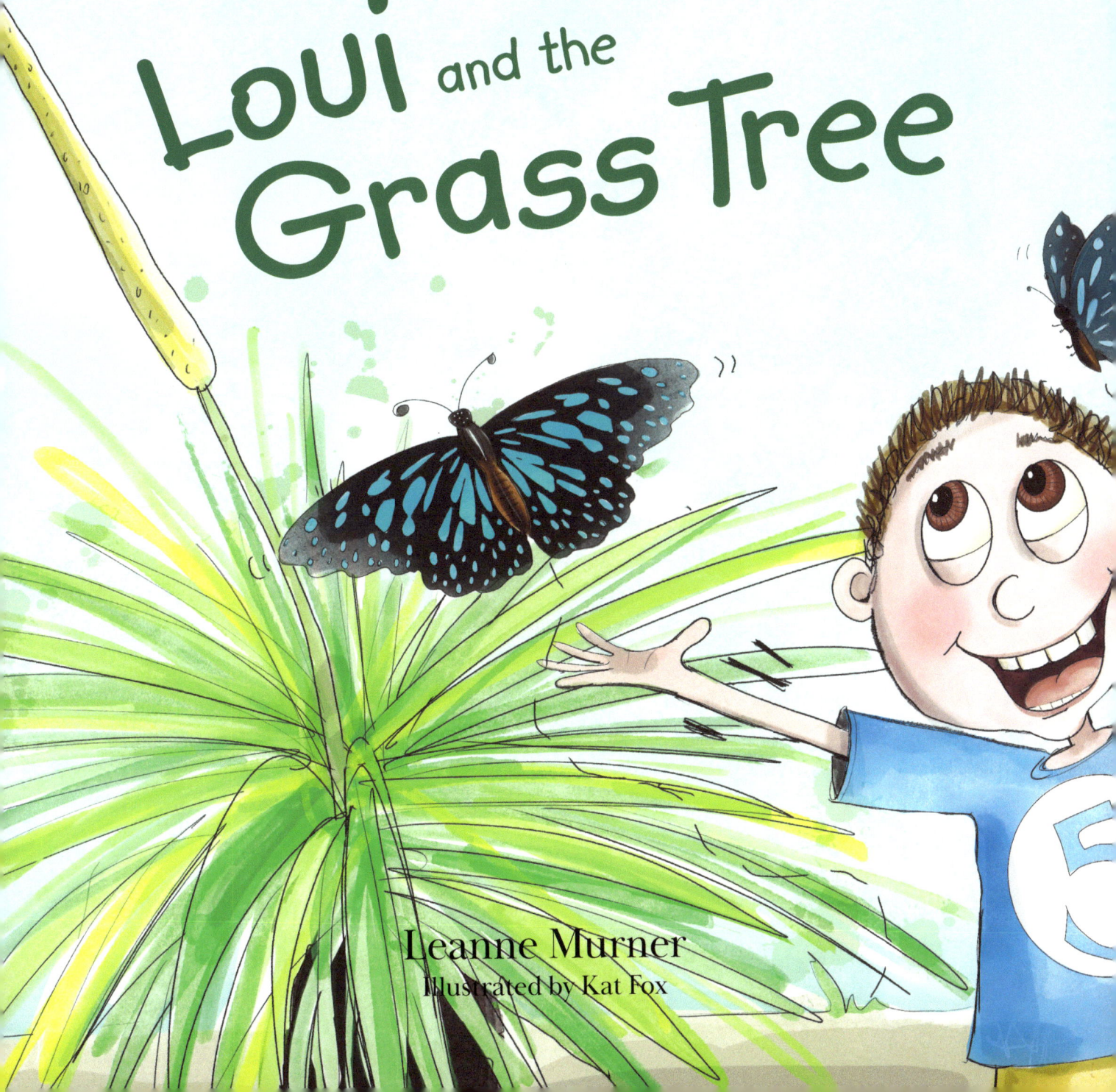

Leanne Murner

Illustrated by Kat Fox

Serenity Press Pty Ltd
Waikiki, WA 6169

First published by Serenity Press (Serenity Press Kids) in 2020
www.serenitypress.org

National Library of Australia
Cataloguing in-Publication entry

Murner, Leanne (Leanne, Murner), Louis and the Grass Tree

ISBN: 978-0-6450996-5-2 (sc)
ISBN: 978-0-6451307-6-8 (hc)

Loui and the Grass Tree

Leanne Murner

Illustrated by Kat Fox

Loui and his family were out
for a bush walk.
"Loui" said Poppy John,
"Come and look at what I
found!"

Poppy John turned around and
Loui was gone!
"Loui! Loui!" yelled Poppy John,
 "Where are you?"

Poppy John could hear
giggling from over under
the tree.
"Loui what are you doing?"
"Hiding" said Loui.
"Oh, you are under the grass
tree" said Poppy John.

"All that grass looks like the tree's hair"
said Loui.
"Yes Loui" Poppy John said,
"See all these new little shoots coming
out here you can pull these out and eat
them. These leaves are very sharp so be
careful Loui, these can be used as a knife,
they are also dried out and used to weave
baskets. These plants have so many uses
for the aboriginal people"

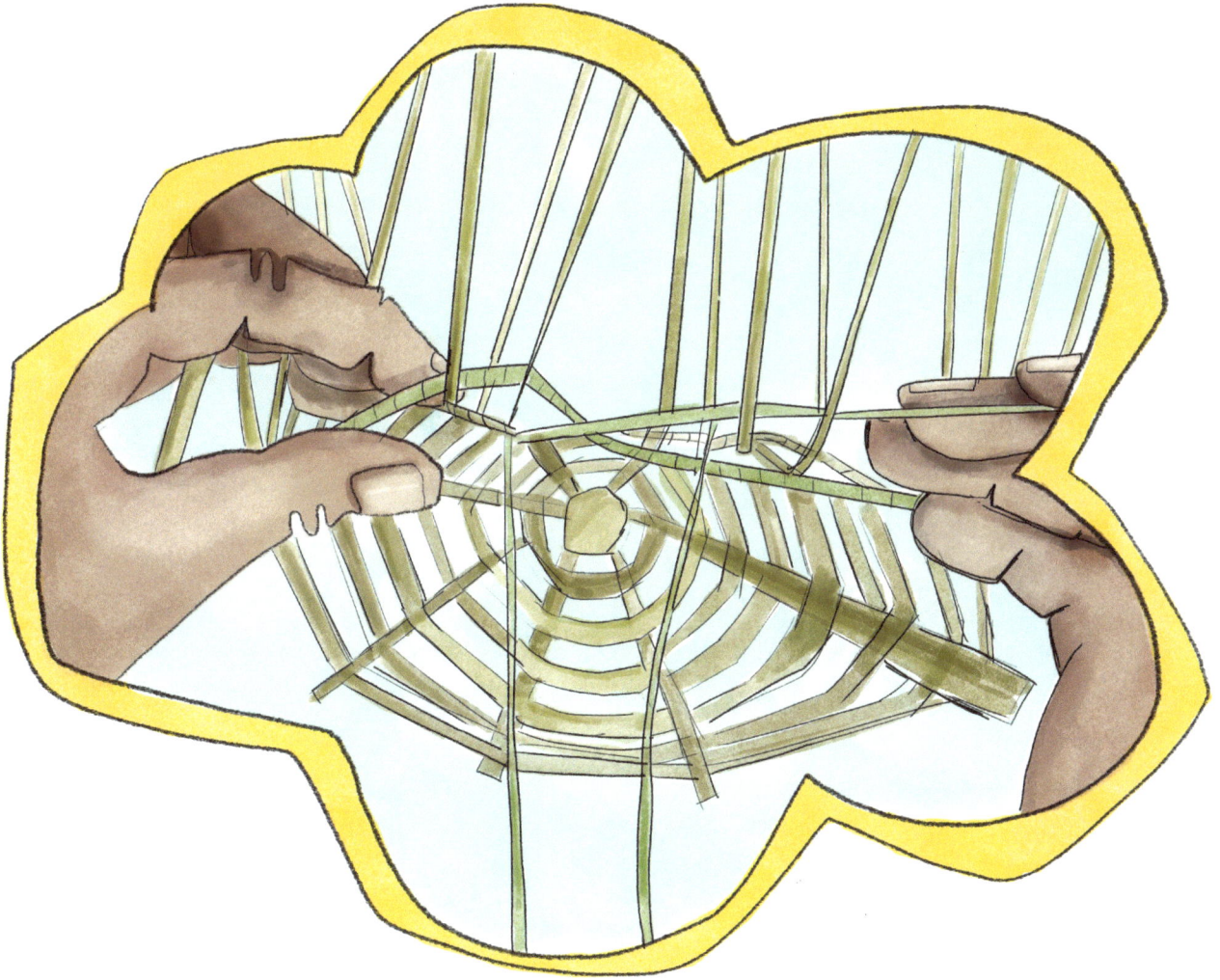

"Why is the trunk all black Poppy?"

"This grass tree has been through a fire and it has left the trunk all burnt, these plants rely on fire to help burn away the old leaves" said John.

"Oh, Poppy John what is this coming out of the trunk, it looks all sticky" said Loui.

"That is a sap that the tree produces, this is used as a glue for spears or fill holes in canoes." said Poppy John

"What do they use the spears for Poppy?" said Loui.

"They use them to hunt for food."

"That is a big spike Poppy John"
said Loui.
This is what aboriginal people use
for their spears, they also use it to
make fire" said Poppy John.
"Fire" said Loui.
"Yes Loui pass it here and I will
show you" said John.

"When the spike dries out all these little pods open and drop thousands of little seeds onto the ground. The spike can grow in heaps of different directions not just straight up" said Poppy John.

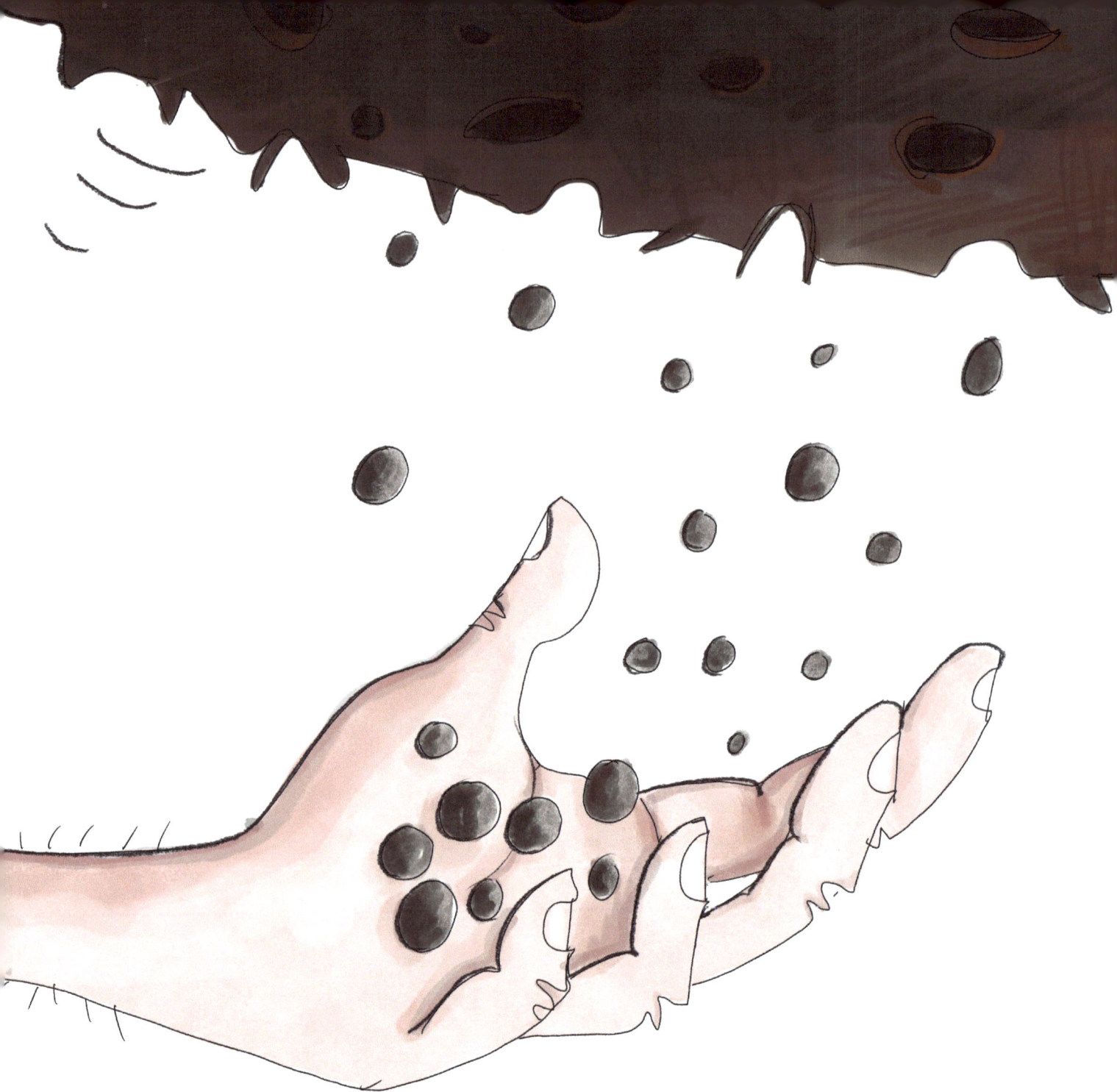

"Loui have a look at these, they are the seeds
from the spike" said Poppy John.
"Can I take them home Poppy?" Loui asks.
"Yes, Loui you could go and plant these seeds
and grow your own grass tree."

"Oh, Poppy John what is that butterfly doing?"
said Loui.
"It's going in for a drink, birds, insects and
honey gliders come and drink the nectar from
the flowers" said Poppy John.

"Mum"

"Dad"

"Look what I have found" said Loui.

"Hey Mum?" said Loui,
"Can I take some seeds to show my class and tell them
about the grass tree I found?" said Loui.
"Yes Loui, what a great idea" said mum.

Bee (Green Carpenter Bee)

The Green Carpenter Bee is a large iconic native bee species. It is beautiful jewel, metallic green in colour, and is friendly and harmless. The species is extinct on mainland South Australia and Victoria but still exists on Kangaroo Island, and around Sydney and the Great Dividing Range in NSW.

These dazzling bees probably became extinct in these areas because fires and land clearing destroyed their nest sites. There is concern that remaining Carpenter Bee populations on Kangaroo Island, SA, continue to decline.

These species rely on soft wood to make its nests they dig nest burrows inside dry flower spikes of Xanthorrhoea grass trees or in soft dead trunks of Banksia.

Butterfly (Blue Tiger Butterfly)

The Blue Tiger is a delight to the eye. They have a wingspan of 75 to 105 mm. The head, antennae and thorax is brownish black in colour, with white dots on the head and neck. The Blue Tiger Butterflies have brownish black upperparts, with bluish white semi hyaline spots and streaks.

They feed mostly on toxic plants, fly slowly and spend long periods resting in sheltered areas during winter.

Their pupa is fresh green and shiny with some golden spots.

Blue Tiger Butterflies can sometimes migrate from North Queensland to Brisbane and have been reported to migrate north every end of March and April, with clouds of them flying right along the coastline from Caloundra to Noosa.

Silvereye Bird

Silvereyes are extremely easy to recognise. They have a ring of white or silvery feathers in a ring around their eyes. Silvereyes look a little different, depending on where they come from in Australia, but generally they have olive green and grey feathers.

They might only grow to about 15 cm tall and weigh only 5-10 g, but the hardy Silvereye has amazing life span. Silvereyes can live for up to ten years, which is a long time for such a tiny bird. They can also fly extremely long distances when they migrate at the end of summer.

Silvereyes mainly eat insects, fruit, and nectar.

Grass Tree (Xanthorrhoea)

Grass trees are not a grass or a tree, their trunks are made up of tightly packed leaves. They can take 20 years to flower, growing stalks covered in hundreds of tiny nectar-rich, creamy-white flowers which can grow up to 4 metres long.

The grass tree can recover quickly after a fire thanks to reserves of starch stored in their stem. By examining the size of a grass tree's skirt, we can estimate when a fire last occurred. The can live for up to 600 years, surviving both bush fire and drought.

Flowering is not dependent on fire, but it speeds up the process. The ability of grass trees to resprout after fire and quickly produce flowers makes them a vital lifeline for fauna living in recently-burnt landscapes.

Grass trees provide food for birds, insects, and mammals, which feast on the nectar, pollen, and seeds. Beetle larvae living within the flower spikes are a delicacy for cockatoos. Invertebrates such as green carpenter bees build nests inside the hollowed out scapes of flowers. Honey can be collected from flower stems containing the hives of carpenter bees. Small native mammals become more abundant where grass trees are found, for the dense, unburnt skirt of leaves around the trunk provides shelter and sites for nesting.

Honey Glider Possum

Sugar Gliders have a twin membrane that stretches from their little finger to their hind legs. When fully stretched out in flight they act as a wing or a parachute enabling them to glide across open areas in the trees. They have another use for these membrane wings. When they forage, they use them as pockets to collect food in to take back to their young.

These small marsupials live in eastern and northern Australia and nest in tree hollows or nest boxes. Adults can weigh as little as 150 grams. They are grey to brown with a prominent dark stripe over their foreheads and have prehensile tails which they use to grip on to branches.

In June, Sugar Gliders begin mating. The female will soon give birth to two babies which are independent by 10 months old.

As they are only 15 cm long and weigh up to just 150g, Sugar Gliders only need a small entrance to their nest which helps them feel safe from predators.

Sugar Gliders are social animals and will share their new home with several adult gliders and their infants. If warning off predators, you will hear them emit a series of shrill barks.

Sugar gliders especially like forests with an understory of acacia, the sap of which they devour. They also eat acacia seeds, nectar, pollen and invertebrates.

Dedication

I would like to dedicate this book to my best friend and husband.
Thank you for supporting me through this amazing journey.

My 5 little men being my inspiration, Poppy John for his wealth of
knowledge and support.

And to my amazing friend Amy for pushing me out of my comfort zone
two years ago, starting my new life purpose.

I would not be here today without you believing in me.

About the Author

Leanne Murner is an author, business owner/designer at 5 Little Bears Pty Ltd and a proud mum of 5 boys. Leanne saw a gap in the market for Australian themed wooden toys and began creating products for children with an educational and Australian twist. Being a creative soul Leanne grew the business fast and as time went by her product portfolio increased. In Addition she has also published the first of a series of 6 children's books, Franki and the Banskia with the remaining being published this year. Leanne wanted to teach kids about Australian native flora and fauna, what they are and who needs them to survive. Leanne is busy working an another series of books teaching kids about Australian animals and their habitat, threats and how we can help. Leanne is passionate that our children need to be better educated on Australian wildlife to help from extinction.

9780645130768